Praise for *Amy's Travels*

"*Amy's Travels* is a delightful adventure of a little girl who moves with her family every few years to a different continent. This appealing journey enables children to obtain a broad perspective of the world as seen through the eyes of Amy, the central character. By focusing on each of the seven continents, the reader is able to conceptualize both their vast differences and stark similarities. Beautifully written and magnificently illustrated, *Amy's Travels* is the perfect selection for teachers when developing children's background experiences for Social Studies at any grade level."

— Dr. Katherine Wisendanger, Professor, Literacy and Culture Program, Longwood University

"Written by second grade teacher Kathryn Starke, *Amy's Travels* is a softcover children's picturebook that invites young readers to accompany Amy along her trip to all seven of Earth's continents. From the rainforest jungles of Africa to the mountains of South America and the cultured cities of Europe, *Amy's Travels* offers a child's eye view of the delights of encountering new people, places, and cultures. Simple color drawings on every other page add a unique touch of charm to this storybook, especially recommended for sharing with children before a family trip."

—*The Midwest Book Review*

"*Amy's Travels* is a wonderful story about a young girl who has visited each of the continents. The story is based on the life of author Kathryn Starke's friend Amy. Not only does this book provide a window into each of the continents, it also provides lesson plans and activities for grades K-5. This book provides an opportunity for students who otherwise would never have the chance to visit any other continent."

— Alison Perry, Elementary School Teacher, Richmond, Virginia

Amy's Travels

by Kathryn Starke

Illustrations by
Jennifer Carter
Charity Wells
and Laura Starke

To Cate–
May you always enjoy your travels
through reading! Thanks for joining the CMP
team!
Kathryn Starke
6/2/19

Creative Minds Publications
Richmond, Virginia

www.creativemindspublications.com

ISBN 0-9769737-3-1
LCCN 2011960081

Creative Minds Publications
2325 Crowncrest Drive
Richmond, Virginia 23233
804.740.6010
www.creativemindspublications.com
info@creativemindspublications,com

Thank you to Amy Kramer, the real life version of our main character.

This book is dedicated to my mom and dad,
Kay and Jay Starke, and my two sisters,
Elizabeth and Laura Starke.

School
School Bus

Hi, I'm Amy, and ever since I was a tiny baby, I have loved to travel. My dad has a job that allows him to move every few years to a brand new place. I have been to lots of different schools, made lots of friends, and packed a ton of suitcases. My dad, mom, big brother, and I have lived all around the world.

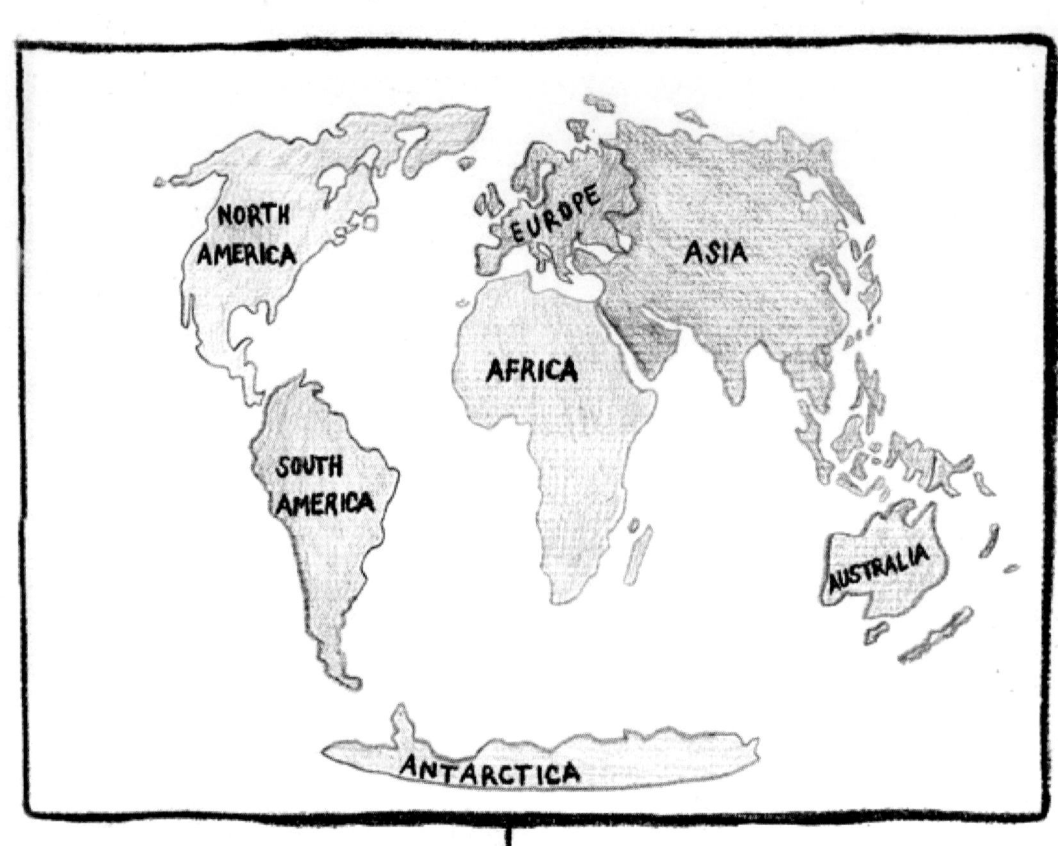
NORTH AMERICA
EUROPE
ASIA
AFRICA
SOUTH AMERICA
AUSTRALIA
ANTARCTICA

There are seven continents in the world. Continents are very large areas of land. They are North America, South America, Europe, Asia, Africa, Australia, and Antarctica. My family has lived on five of the seven continents.

There is one continent that my family has never even tried to move to. No family can live there because it is too cold to survive. Have you ever met anyone who lives in Antarctica? The continent Antarctica is located on the southern tip of Earth. It is the coldest place in the world, so it remains the home to penguins and glaciers, which are huge sheets of ice.

I was born in Peru, just like my mom. Peru is a country on the continent of South America. When I was only a few days old, I made my first move to our new home in Honduras. I was a good baby, and I loved playing with my big brother. My first word was Mami, which means mom in Spanish. Spanish is the language I learned when I was little.

Jambo. That means hello in Swahili, the native language of Kenya. We moved to this country on the continent of Africa when I was three years old. I went to kindergarten in Kenya. My school was made up of lots of small huts. The students used a different hut for lunch, music, or library.

My favorite thing about living in Africa was going on a safari. My big brother and I would climb into a high jeep and ride through the tall grasses in the wildlife. We watched lions, zebras, and hippopotamuses wandering around the grasses. They are not in cages like in the zoo because the jungle is their home.

I bet you go to the beach when you have summer vacation from school! Well, my family travels to Europe. Europe is another continent located to the north of Africa. It is a small continent with lots of different countries, many different types of people, and many languages. We visited a beautiful country called Holland which is famous for its hills and windmills. Windmills were built a long time ago to pump water. Today some of the windmills have been turned into restaurants, where my family would go out to dinner.

Remember when I told you I was born in South America? Well, I moved away for a while, but I moved back to Peru when I was in third grade. A large part of Peru is the Amazon Rain Forest. The jungle is large, hot, very rainy, and a home to a large number of animals. The neatest thing about this place is that at night you can take a canoe ride on the Amazon River to see monkeys, bat caves, and frogs. You can even feel the crocodiles swimming under the canoe!

I did not move to the United States of America in North America until I was eleven years old, and I still live here. We live in the state of Virginia close to Washington D.C. The coolest thing about the United States is that they have four seasons-fall, spring, summer, and winter. In other places around the world, the weather is either dry or rainy. I experienced my first snow day when I lived in America! Now I look forward to snow every winter.

The largest continent on earth is Asia. My dad's job just transferred him to Asia, where he will learn a new area and meet brand new people. I plan to make a trip to Asia this summer. Asia includes lots of countries with mountains and flat land, but my dad will be living in the desert where it is hot and dry. It is a land of sand where camels are a form of transportation.

The next place I want to explore is the continent of Australia, which is known as the "land down under." Kangaroos and koalas are the native animals, and you can scuba dive into the Great Coral Reef. It will be another adventure for me to explore. I have learned so much through my travels around the world, and each continent has something special to offer. So, what continent will you visit first?

Lesson Plans
for *Amy's Travels*

Created by
Kathryn Starke

As an elementary school literacy specialist, I am always looking for new children's books to add to the curriculum in the classroom. I wrote *Amy's Travels* when I taught second grade to provide an educational material to teach the seven continents, geography, and global awareness. I encourage you to use the following kindergarten-fifth grade lesson plans with your students. In addition, a downloadable comprehensive book guide is available at www.creativemindspublications.com

Kindergarten

Objective: to use positional words to describe relative locations of places

Activity: During reading, each child will hold an index card with certain positional words to show what they think about the location of the seven continents.

Position Words: near/far;
above/below;
left/right;
behind/in front

Example: Is South America above or below North America?

First Grade

Objective: to interpret the cardinal directions on a map

Activity: Before reading, each child will take a paper plate and label the cardinal directions (north, south, east, west) in the proper location and make a paper arrow for the center of the plate to make a compass.

During reading, the children will use the compass to show which direction Amy is traveling.

Second Grade

Objective: to label and identify the seven continents around the world

Activity: After reading, the teacher will use clues and information from the story to create fact cards that the children will choose from a pile to play "Guess My Continent."

Example: This continent is full of glaciers. (Antarctica)

Third Grade

Objective: to recognize the shape and position of the seven continents

Activity: During reading, the children can use a counter or object on a blank world map to follow the route of Amy's travels.

After reading, the children can label the world map by memory and check

Fourth Grade

Objective: to locate Virginia on a map and understand Virginia history

Activity: Amy moved to Virginia when she moved to the continent of North America. Create a postcard to send to Amy. Write and draw a historical place or event that she would see in Virginia.

Examples: Jamestown, Williamsburg, Monticello, etc.

Fifth Grade

Objective: to understand different perspectives around
the world

Activity: The children can compare and contrast his or her own travels and traditions around the United States and the world to Amy's travels. Each child can fold a piece of paper in half to write and illustrate the travels that he or she chooses.

Example: Amy has been to Europe. I have been to Disney World.